First paperback edition July 2022

Illustrations by Oleg Kravets

ISBN 979-8-9865463-1-5 (paperback)
ISBN 979-8-9865463-0-8 (e-book)

www.teampbj.net

CONTENTS

INTRODUCTION
FREE-DONUT FRIDAYS

When Dr. Vile rolled into town on his super green-goo machine, his really bad haircut blowing in the breeze behind him like a wet rag, he had only one thought in mind: *take over the world.* Of course, he was also thinking about the juicy-looking tacos he had just passed, but this was no time for tacos. Besides, Dr. Vile could just make food—any kind of food—using his green-goo zapper. It was all part of his nasty plan.

Now, getting zapped with goo might sound like fun to you, but this goo changes you into food, and any kind of food Dr. Vile wants. Including hamburgers.

1

The evil scientist wasn't afraid of anyone, though he was afraid of some *things*: kittens, especially the soft, cute, cuddly ones, but thankfully no one knew that (or at least, not yet). Dr. Vile had always been terrified of the little furballs, and every time his family sent him photos of Alex or Agatha, Stripey or Sylvester, he had to delete their texts forever.

Let's just say he deleted a *lot* of texts.

But really, if any cute kitten ever tried to get near him or even meow from a distance, he would just zap it with his famous green goo. Dr. Vile smiled at the idea of turning a tiny kitten into a hamburger with French fries.

Yes, he really was that evil.

Anyway, Dr. Vile—the smartest scientist in the world—wasn't in town for hamburgers, kittens, or tacos.

He was here to take over the galaxy, starting in the smallest town he could find: Goodsprings.

I don't even think Google Maps knows about Goodsprings, and I've never heard of Amazon making any deliveries there. In fact, the town is so far off the highway that most people have forgotten where the highway even *is*. Maybe someday they'll find it again.

When Dr. Vile stopped at Goodsprings, he laughed and got out his green-goo zapper. It was only a matter of time before he controlled this tiny little town and turned the cars into chocolate pudding.

Slowly, slowly, Dr. Vile drove down Main Street, looking in every direction for his target: Town Hall and the mayor. Get the mayor, and you get Goodsprings. Get Goodsprings, and you get the taco stand (he *really* wanted those juicy tacos).

Finally, his machine pulled into town square. It had been a long drive from his deep, dark cave—also in the middle of nowhere—and Dr. Vile needed a stretch. He got out, cracked his flimsy arms and legs, then sat down and calmly clipped his toenails on the sidewalk.

Everyone was watching from their windows. *Is he going to clean those toenails up?* they all thought.

No. No he wasn't.

SUPERHERO TIP #1: BEWARE OF BAD GUYS WHO CLIP THEIR TOENAILS. IT MEANS THEY ARE SUPER WELL-ORGANIZED AND HAVE EXTRA TIME FOR CONQUERING STUFF.

After combing his wet-rag hair and looking in a mirror (he had to look good for the big moment), Dr. Vile pressed a tiny button on his white lab coat. His screechy voice rang out on the loudest microphone Goodsprings had ever heard.

"Um—yes—good day to you people. My name is Dr. Edwin Vile, and I am here to take over, well—*your town*— and then the universe. Bwahaha!"

By now the town's two old security guards, Ron and Phil, had arrived and were hiding behind telephone poles seven blocks away. They held their breath and waited. *Who was this guy? And would he take away free-donut Fridays?*

The mayor, Bobby Lumford, stepped out from the town bank and shouted, "You'll never take our donuts from us! We've got a superhero on our side!"

Dr. Vile laughed and shook his head. "I don't *care* about your superhero, you overgrown pizza stick!"

Still half-snickering, half-coughing on his own saliva, Dr. Vile whipped out a long, gray remote and pointed it right at the mayor. "Want a drink, mayor?" A flash of green light lit up the main square, and a delivery truck filled with frozen foods turned instantly into a mega-sized strawberry milkshake.

The mayor licked his lips. "Um, Mr. Dr. Vile, is that milkshake for me? And did you say *pizza sticks*?"

So that's how, in just a few seconds, Dr. Vile became lord of Goodsprings. And if everything went according to plan, it wouldn't be long before he was king of the universe.

CHAPTER 1

A SUPER LAME SUPERPOWER

My name's Christolpherson Rederson, and I'm a fifth-grade student at Goodsprings Elementary School. It's a pretty cool school, but not if you have the weirdest first and last name in the entire universe, like I do. I think the name Hippo Head Jr. would have been better.

You're probably thinking, *Christolpherson Rederson?! Did your parents name you when they were five years old? Or did a monkey pick your name?*

Yeah, yeah, I know. And as if that's not bad enough—well, I've got a terrible secret.

I'm a superhero.

Being a superhero is normally a wonderful thing. I mean, just look at how popular Spiderman is. The guy's got like twenty movies. And that red Spidey suit is sick. To make it even cooler, he got bit by a spider on a field trip. *A field trip!* Ultimate proof that every school day should be a fun, recreational, and dangerous learning activity.

SUPERHERO TIP #2: ALWAYS LET A SPIDER OR TWO BITE YOU ON FIELD TRIPS. YOU NEVER KNOW WHEN IT WILL BE YOUR LUCKY DAY.

In the movies, superhero work is always exciting. There's this great moment when the hero saves a falling girl and they fly off into the sunset and it's—just—*exciting.* A hundred percent cooler than my life.

You wanna know what my lame-o superpower is? Well, I don't talk about it very much, since most people think it's super weird, and I'm one of them. The only people who don't think I'm lame are Mom, Dad, my best friend, Jimmy, and Jimmy's little brother, Randy. But unfortunately, my parents' love blinds them to the truth, and Jimmy can make his thumbs do this weird double-jointed thing, and let's not even mention Randy (he bites). Need more proof that I'm totally lame?

Okay, so here goes.

Like I said, I warned you.

My superpower is making peanut butter and jelly sandwiches fly out of my hands.

THERE! I said it. Making unlimited PB&Js is my superpower, plain and simple.

So at this point, most people are on the ground laughing so hard they can't breathe. And I don't blame them, because if I was somebody else, I'd also be rolling around gasping for air.

But anyway, probably the worst part of having super-PB&J strength is Sophia Little. Boy oh boy, did I get off on the wrong foot with Sophia.

It all happened the same day I found out about my superpowers. I mean, it was my *moment*, that part of the movie when the hero finds the Batcave and realizes his destiny and all that. This was my time to shine . . . or so I thought.

It was first grade and it was lunchtime. Our class was waiting in line at the cafeteria. Jimmy was standing right beside me, chatting casually to me about robots or something while my belly made a really loud rhino grumble. Sophia Little was right in front of us, and when she heard the rhino rumble, she rolled her eyes and inched away from me.

Quick sidenote about BFF Jimmy: like I said, unusual thumbs, but he's also the smartest kid in town. He's helped me out a thousand times with my long-division homework because he says it's "mentally stimulating" (I had to use a dictionary for that one). The funny part, or maybe the sad part for me (you'll have to decide by the end of this story), is he's *really* clumsy. You know, always running into people and telephone poles and kiddy slides and stuff.

Now, usually it's safe to reach out for a plate of food, right? Well, that's what I thought. There I was, putting out my hands to take a plate of chicken fingers and mashed potatoes from the lunch lady, when suddenly a perfectly formed PB&J sandwich shot out of my hands and hit Sophia right in the back of the head.

Sophia, her head now miraculously transformed into a huge, dripping peanut-ball smear and mountain of strawberry-jelly drizzle, turned and, with narrow, dark eyes more terrifying than I could possibly imagine, slowly peeled the sandwich off her head and smooshed it—no, jammed it—straight up my nostrils.

For a few seconds, all I could breathe was peanuts (they did smell pretty good, all things considered), but then the whole lunchroom broke into laughter, and I did the only thing I could as a first grader with a newly discovered superpower and a sandwich stuck up his nose—I ran for it.

That was my big mistake. I didn't realize that running with a PB&J on your face blocks your senses. Also, my superpower just decided it was time to come out and see the world.

With my hands out in front of me, searching desperately for a way to escape the sea of howling, whooping faces (my sense of hearing unfortunately was still working just fine), I accidentally started sending sandwiches in every direction.

And I mean *every* direction.

Principal McNeal heard the hooting and snorting from the hallway and had just stepped into the lunchroom to see what the hubbub was, when he got hit with a mega couch-sized PB&J that rocked him right on the bottom and sent him careening into a screaming pile of eleven-year-old girls.

All that to say: the first day of my professional career as PB&Spray Boy, the name lovingly given to me by Sophia from that day forward and adopted by the entire school and then the entire town, was also the last day of my life as a superhero. After that, I just wanted to hide.

Like I said, fifth grade at Goodsprings Elementary School is great, just not if you're me. And that's because I have the weirdest superpower ever.

CHAPTER 2

DEAD MEAT

So when Dr. Vile rolled into town and became "Lord Vile of the Universe," I knew my time had come. I wasn't just doomed to be the school joke—I was *dead meat*. Plain and simple. Fried pork on a stick.

As waves of terror crashed over me, I cried in the bathroom at my house. Jimmy (who had just tripped over nothing at all and landed on his face by the bathroom door) tried to calm me down.

"You can do this, PB&J. You're a superhero with a real superpower. You can beat this villain, even with his highly developed machine and remarkably transformative green-goo spray."

I tried to find comfort in Jimmy's words, at least the words I could understand, but it was no use. Suddenly, I was back in first grade, running from Sophia, knocking over the principal, and getting tackled to the ground by the librarian, Mrs. Hunt, who held her sides and laughed at me with a face like a red balloon.

With my head over the sink in case I threw up, I started to cry again. Pathetic, right? Just what everybody wants from their superhero.

But maybe Jimmy had a point. I mean, I *was* a superboy, even if I was lame. I could do something no one else could. I took another look in the mirror, wiped the snot from my red, puffy face, and opened the door.

Jimmy was still on the ground, only now he had a rugburn shaped like an alien head on his cheek. He smiled at me weakly and struggled to his feet.

I took one look at that alien head and started panicking again. Pushing my way back to the bathroom for another cry session, I said to him, "Jimmy, I really don't think I can do this. I mean, making PB&Js is *fun* stuff. I'd be like the best superhero ever for a kid's birthday party. Those little ankle biters could just eat and smoosh sandwiches into their faces all day long."

Jimmy looked at me blankly. Maybe "ankle biters" reminded him too much of his little brother, Randy.

"But defeating a super villain?" I continued, shaking my head. "He's gonna turn me into a bean burrito!"

Jimmy suddenly snapped back to reality. "I *love* bean burritos," he said.

"Exactly," I said. "He'll turn me into a burrito, and you can eat me. Case closed."

After I finally pulled it together, we went into the kitchen to find some juice. My mom and dad were watching the morning news.

"Hey, guys!" They were both talking in high voices and had big smiles on their faces, like they were actors in a terrible show for toddlers.

There was an awkward pause. Jimmy tripped on the back of my shoe and hit the counter, producing a strange mooing sound.

Suddenly, Mom spoke her mind. Her voice was cracked and high-pitched. From my ten years of experience with Mom, she was also about to start crying at any second— and I'm talking thunderstorm tears, not just a light cry like my bathroom experience. I braced for the worst and considered grabbing an umbrella.

"Now listen, boys. Don't go outside, okay? This Dr. What's-His-Face looks dangerous, and he has a really bad haircut too. Creepy looking guy. Your dad's already barred the doors and windows. You just let the police handle it all."

"But Mom," I cut in, surprised to find myself suddenly so fearless, "Jimmy has a bad haircut too, but that doesn't make him dangerous! And what police are you talking about? Do you mean Ron and Phil? They're like eighty-five years old!"

Jimmy nodded in agreement. The last time he went for a haircut, Randy had tickled the hairdresser and made her snip a huge chunk out of Jimmy's 'do. To cover up this gaping hole of horror, he's been wearing a baseball hat, but today I hid it under my bed when he wasn't looking just to see what he would do. So far, he's just absentmindedly scratched his head and mumbled, "I wonder where that got to."

"Look, son," said Dad, jumping in. "You've got your whole career as a superhero ahead of you. Dr. Vile isn't a *game*. He'll blast you into chocolate cake if he gets the chance!"

Jimmy licked his lips as he thought about chocolate cake. I punched him in the arm (there were more mooing sounds) and said to Dad, "But no one else will save the town if I don't! You already saw what happened this morning—the mayor surrendered without a fight! All he wanted was a milkshake, for goodness sake!"

"That's all part of their plan to beat Mr. What's-His-Face, honey," said Mom. "Let the grown-ups figure it out. But you're so sweet to want to help."

Quick as a flash, she moved in for a hug, and before I knew it I was being crushed by a mom death hug. She's famous for them around town. At one point there was actually a petition to outlaw her hugging anyone (don't tell her, but I totally signed it).

While the death squeeze was rearranging my organs, I did have time to think about my situation, and somehow it was a relief that my parents weren't letting me save the universe.

The TV interrupted our sweet embrace as a news report noisily filled the room. Mom released me from her grip, and I almost passed out on the carpet as fresh air swiftly filled my lungs.

SUPERHERO TIP #3: DON'T LET MY MOM SQUISH YOU INTO A WEIRD SHAPE AND FORCE YOU TO LIVE IN A DAYCARE FOR THE REST OF YOUR LIFE.

The reporter was in the middle of saying, "We now have more news from Goodsprings Town Hall. Dr. Edwin Vile is now calling himself Lord Vile." My mother gave a shriek as the totally gross picture of Dr. Vile's ugly monkey face and wet-rag hair flashed across the screen.

"Mr. Dr. Lord Vile is now on the hunt for the superboy Christolpherson Rederson, also known as PB&Spray." After the reporter read my superhero name, he burst into laughter and fell out of his chair.

This is what I mean about being a lame superhero with a weird name. No one takes you seriously, even when you're being hunted down by a crazy scientist. Also, thanks to Sophia, if my name wasn't PB&Spray before, it totally was now.

The reporter, tears still streaming down his face, managed to climb back into his seat and continue talking.

"If anyone knows the location of PB&Spray"—he started howling with laughter again, and there was another ten-second break while he spun around in his chair in tears—"please call Town Hall at the number on the screen. We believe this superboy is dangerous. A $5,000 dollar reward is being offered for PB&Spray's capture . . ." The reporter collapsed in laughter and the news report cut off.

"You're dangerous?" My father asked, confused by all the laughing.

"They're arresting my sweet little Christolpherson?!" my mother screamed, crushing me in yet another death hug.

"Jimmy, help! Death—hug—" was all I could say with limited airflow.

My friend, his eyes still off in bean-burrito land, did some fast Tex-Mex thinking.

"*FREE TACOS!*" he shouted and pointed out the window.

Mom and Dad turned to look, licking their lips, while Jimmy and I ran for it.

CHAPTER 3

THE GREEN GOO

It's not very nice having your whole hometown try to arrest you, especially when half your town knows exactly where you live. Within seconds of the news about a cash reward, our home was surrounded by a bunch of freeloaders still in their pajamas and sipping coffee.

Jimmy and I had boogied out of there faster than I thought was possible for Jimmy to run. A few minutes later, we were deep in the woods and safely inside our poorly constructed but cozy fort. The fort was basically a few scraps of warped wood that Jimmy had found in the dumpster and thought were "an incredible example of hard-oak boards."

He has such a beautiful way with words.

SUPERHERO TIP #4: YOUR FORT SHOULD ALWAYS BE HARD TO FIND, BUT NOT SO HARD THAT YOU FORGET WHERE IT IS.

Jimmy was also the world's leading kid expert on tech stuff. That was good, because I was totally clueless about computers. One time I asked Jimmy to help me fix my broken laptop. I had spent all afternoon messing around with it, but he found the problem in two seconds.

"You have to plug it in," Jimmy said.

"I knew that already," I said, then ran to the bathroom for a good cry (this happens often).

Anyway, when we got to our fort, Jimmy showed me something new he had been working on.

"It's a surveillance drone," he said excitedly. "And—" he added, grinning like a baboon with missing hair—"look where it is right now!" He mashed a red button on his tablet, and suddenly a live video feed of Town Hall and Dr. Vile's machine popped up on the screen.

I whistled and turned to Jimmy. "Sick!" I slapped him on the back, and his puny body fell out of his chair and landed facedown. Next to the alien-head rugburn there was now a fresh one in the shape of a cow.

"Oops, sorry," I said. "How 'bout a snack?"

Jimmy was back on his feet in a flash. "I'd like two peanut butter and jelly sandwiches on white bread, please."

I put out my hands, and just like that—*poof!*—two perfect PB&Js landed on the table (it was really a cardboard box) behind us.

Taking a mammoth bite and smacking his lips, Jimmy looked down again at his tablet.

I let out a loud yelp. "Where's the drone going?" I was nervous because I was always breaking techy stuff, like the time I accidentally melted my mom's new smartphone on the kitchen burner. There were no death hugs for *weeks* after that.

Jimmy swallowed and said calmly, "I've programmed the drone to follow Dr. Vile. Let's find out what the scientist is devising." He smiled, and I watched him in awe as he sent the drone down the large brick chimney of Town Hall and out into the mayor's office. Once inside, the drone flew to an empty shelf and waited.

Suddenly, a large man with bright red hair burst into the room.

"It's Mayor Lumford!" I shouted.

Right behind the mayor was Dr. Vile with a strange, crazy smile on his monkey face. Now that I saw him up close, I realized how ugly he was—like a white lemur that had never taken his chewy kid vitamins. His arms were weak and flabby, too. I think Jimmy could have beat him in arm wrestling, and that was saying something, because even Randy, who was three years old, had beaten Jimmy once (I was there when it happened, and it wasn't a pretty sight).

Dr. Vile stood in the doorway and was waving around what looked like a big remote. I could tell that he was angry.

"Tell me where the superboy is!" the evil scientist shouted at the mayor.

"Can you say 'please'? I need you to be more polite before I can help you," said Mayor Lumford, trembling with fear and politeness.

SUPERHERO TIP #5: ALWAYS TEACH THE BAD GUYS TO SAY "PLEASE" AND "THANK YOU" BEFORE YOU DEFEAT THEM.

"Okay, fine! *Please* tell me where the superboy is," answered Dr. Vile.

"I don't know!" was Mayor Lumford's unhelpful reply. "If he's not at home, I guess you could check the school."

"It's Saturday—*there is no school!*" said Dr. Vile angrily.

"Oh, yeah . . . can I have another hamburger now?" asked the mayor.

"Of course I'm going to give you another hamburger! Bwahaha! Eat your heart out!" said Dr. Vile, who pressed a button on his big zapper thingy.

Something like green goo exploded in the air, and a delicious-looking hamburger and French fries appeared where the desk chair used to be.

"Go ahead, Mayor Lumford. Take a *bite*," said Dr. Vile menacingly.

Mayor Lumford hesitated for less than a second, then reached out and stuffed the entire hamburger into his mouth in one chomp.

"No way he just did that," I said, in awe of both the green goo and our monster mayor.

Back on the video feed, Dr. Vile laughed again. This time it was a crazy laughter that echoed all around the room. Jimmy got so scared that he choked and snorted a low-calorie peanut right out his nose.

As Mayor Lumford moved on to the French fries, Dr. Vile shouted, "The universe is *mine!*"

CHAPTER 4

EVERYTHING JELLY

P B&J, wait—you've got to stop and think about this," said Jimmy at the door to our fort. He looked weird to me for some reason—and then I noticed he had a large jelly smudge across his forehead from where he had tried to smack a fly. The smudge made him look like a big toddler at snack time.

"Jimmy," I said, "I'm done waiting. Mom and Dad were right. Dr. Vile won't stop until he finds me. And I'm the superhero here, remember? Mayor Lumford is in danger. We've got to rescue him!"

I also thought the hamburger and fries combo looked super tasty, but I decided Jimmy wouldn't appreciate that kind of argument. He was more of a taco guy.

"PB&J, don't you understand?" said Jimmy. "I think there's something *in the food*! He's controlling Mayor Lumford with all those hamburgers and milkshakes!"

I felt stunned, especially since it was a real dirty trick to control someone with a hamburger. Broccoli or asparagus, sure. But a *hamburger*? It was Dr. Vile's worst trick yet.

"Okay," I said to Jimmy, "I promise not to eat any hamburgers. Can I go now, *Mom*?"

"Yes, sweetie," Jimmy said in a high-pitched tone, and then opened his arms to squeeze me in a fake death hug. Fake because Jimmy's skinny arms could never hurt a fly (his jelly-smeared face was proof of that).

"Wait, before you go—" As Jimmy rummaged around the room, I saw that his haircutting disaster was even worse in the back. A huge shape like a fist had been cut out of his blond hair. *After we beat Dr. Vile, I'll give Jimmy's baseball hat back. Or buy him a bucket.*

Suddenly, Jimmy whipped around, holding a picture of a very tiny, very cute kitten.

I moaned. "Seriously? This again? As if we're not weird enough already." Jimmy always makes me take a picture of George, his lucky tabby cat, on all official missions.

Then we stood side by side and recited Team PB&J's inspiring chant:

> *Peanuts, butter, and everything nice,*
> *We use PB hands to beat the bad guys!*
> *Peanuts, butter, and everything jelly,*
> *When we don't fight, we fill up our bellies!*

Like I said, real inspiring (Jimmy wrote it, okay?).

After we finished, I left Jimmy behind at the fort to handle the drone while I went to find Dr. Vile.

CHAPTER 5

SOPHIA LITTLE STRIKES BACK

I was still cringing from our team chant when I turned the corner into town. There in front of me were the steep stairs leading up to Town Hall.

The memory of those steps and the seed-spitting contest burst into my brain. Last year, we fourth graders lined up on the top step to see who could spit a watermelon seed the farthest. Sophia was there too, and obviously I really wanted to crush her in style.

Simple, right? Unfortunately, no. I've always had a problem with drooling ("It's because of your sweet baby face," Mom always says), and when it was my turn to spit, the seed got stuck under my tongue. I blew harder, but it only dribbled down my chin, traveling on a wad of drool and landing *behind* me on Mr. Lane's pants.

Blaze Malinski was up next, and his watermelon seed soared twenty steps. *Twenty!* I was so mad that I nailed him with a PB&J that sent *him* flying too (strangely, I've never been allowed to compete again).

Today, though, there were no spitting contests. The steps in front of Town Hall were quiet. In fact, *all* of Main Street was quiet. Too quiet. I slowed from a run to a walk, then stopped and squatted down by a bench. I sniffed the air. No hamburgers anywhere.

Suddenly, a totally random thing happened. There, coming around the corner and heading straight up the steps, was Sophia Little! I gaped at her with an open mouth. Didn't she know the danger she was in?

Not that I cared too much. But once my superhero instincts kick in, I can't stop them.

So in a flash I crossed the street and bolted up the stairs to save Sophia from her green-goo-and-hamburger-with-French-fries fate.

Strangely, I was shouting to her, but somehow she didn't seem to hear me, even though it was totally quiet outside and I used my best superhero voice.

SUPERHERO TIP #6: IF YOU'RE GOING TO BE A SUPERHERO, YOU'VE GOT TO DO THE VOICE. YOU KNOW, THAT LOW, GRUFFY VOICE THAT BATMAN HAS.

My super voice was, sadly, so bad that Sophia didn't seem to notice me at all. She just kept on walking, tossing an apple up and down in her hand and humming to herself.

"SOPHIAAA!" I shouted again, this time giving up the super voice and squawking like a parrot.

But it was no use. She opened the door and walked straight inside Town Hall. I shook my head—this girl was loony bins!

I reached the top of the steps just as the door closed behind her. I paused, then wrenched open the doors and plunged inside, running as fast as I could.

It was cold and dark in Town Hall. Where in the world was Sophia?

The answer to my question came faster than I expected. In the blink of an eye, the lights flicked on, and I found myself surrounded by Dr. Vile, a strange smile on his pimply lemur face, and Sophia Little. *What a traitor!* I said to myself. *Is she seriously still holding a grudge about the PB&J thing from first grade?*

I never in a million years would have believed it was possible for a fifth-grade girl to be so awful to a sweet superhero like me, but here was all the proof I needed. *Should I hit her with a peanut butter on dry toast?* I thought, ready for all-out war, but for some reason I stopped myself.

Dr. Vile had his hand on his green-goo zapper and mashed a button. Where a statue of Ben Franklin had been, there was now a delicious-looking plate of fried chicken and hot mashed potatoes.

My stomach rumbled. *Oof, whoa. When was the last time I ate? Gosh, it's almost 11:30. Breakfast was two hours ago. I can't fight on an empty stomach . . .*

Food! Suddenly, my mind cleared, and I thought about Jimmy. The food—Dr. Vile was controlling everyone with *the food*, and I had almost fallen for his cruel joke.

For the first time, I noticed the apple in Sophia's hand, and I realized that she had already taken a bite. She was already under Dr. Vile's spell.

I'll call her Robot Sophia! I laughed to myself.

I might be a lame superhero, but at least *I* don't work for the bad guy.

SUPERHERO TIP #7: NEVER, EVER, EVER WORK FOR THE BAD GUY.

Suddenly, strangely, I felt a wave of peanut-butter anger come up from my hands. Quick as a flash, Dr. Vile mashed his zapper again, and this time I realized the floor beneath me was turning to jello and I was sinking deeper and deeper into a mushy pool of sweet, delicious squishiness.

My PB&J sandwiches flew out of my hands but totally missed Dr. Vile, hitting the ceiling instead and making a totally gross smiley face as I sank further into the mush.

This jello smells weird, I thought. *Wait, it can't be—is that watermelon flavor?*

My face turned red, and Robot Sophia smiled.

"Remember the seed-spitting contest, PB&Spray?" Sofia said, laughing. I struggled and fought, but the jello was too soft and squishy to escape.

As I sank beneath waves of red jello, I noticed that Dr. Vile wasn't laughing. He was covering his mouth and coughing.

CHAPTER 6

AN UNLIKELY HERO

When I came to, I was lying on the floor of a small room, and I was alone. There was one window, but it was really high up, almost to the ceiling, and I was too tired and desperate with hunger to think about escaping.

Instead, my first thought was to find a bathroom and cry in it, but I knew I could only *truly* cry in my bathroom at home. Those tears are the best tears.

I pulled myself together and sat up.

Just great, I thought. *I'm a prisoner, and it's all because of Sophia. Where is Jimmy and his flying drone, anyway? He would know how to get me out of here . . .*

Just then a door opened, and intense light filled the room. Someone was standing in the doorway, and I was surprised to see it was Robot Sophia.

"Sophia, help me!" I whispered loudly.

"Here's lunch, *superboy*," she said. "Eat it up and stay stwong so you can savey-wavey me, okay?" She set the plate down and whipped around, her hair lashing me in the face.

"Sophia, wait—where's Dr. Vile? What's going on?"

Sophia just stuck out her tongue and headed for the door.

You know, it's a good thing she's being controlled and all, because I really want to drop some big, fat sandwiches on her right now. Also, who says 'stay stwong'? Is that even a thing?

The door slammed shut behind her. My nostrils quickly picked up the scent of my freshly zapped meal.

Mmhmm, lunch. It smells delicious . . . but I'm not gonna fall for it, no sir! Even if I was hungry, I wouldn't eat this. Kind enough to feed me such a tasty and delicious meal, huh? Dr. Vile's trying to control me!

This is how the conversation in my brain was going. And then unfortunately my stomach started thinking for itself.

At first it only grumbled, but then it let out a big rhino growl that rumbled far down in my tummy, the reserve part of the tank I save just for ice cream and sweets. The fact that *this* part of my stomach was empty greatly disturbed me.

The seconds of my captivity were dragging by, and the food was starting to smell better and better.

I started to think, *I've never skipped lunch before. Do you die if you miss a meal?* I leaned in closer to get a glimpse of the spread. *Whoa. A chicken sandwich with chocolate cake for dessert. This is pure torture.*

After about another two or three awfully long seconds of superhero endurance, I decided to try the food out—just one *little bitty* taste. Dr. Vile couldn't control me with one nibble, right?

So, just like that, I gave in to my delicious lunch dream world and shouted at the top of my lungs, "*Oh sweet chicken, come to my mouth!*"

SUPERHERO TIP #8: DON'T TALK TO CHICKENS.

My jaw was just closing around the meat when a loud voice called out, "STOPPP!"

I nearly had a chocolate-cake heart attack from the shock. The sandwich fell from my hands as I quickly looked around me. Was it a ghost? Or worse—Robot Sophia again?

"Who's there?" I whispered under my breath, trying to keep my legs from shaking.

"Up here, in the window—it's *me*!"

Looking down from the window was a very familiar face: *Jimmy!*

"Oh man, am I glad to see you!" I cried.

Jimmy gave me a grin, then slipped, whacking his forehead against the window.

"But how do I get up to you?" I asked, not sure I wanted him to save me after all.

"Use your *sandwiches*!" Jimmy shouted down.

"Sandwiches?!" I said, looking down again at my chicken lunch and licking my lips.

"Build a tower out of PB&Js!" he replied.

"Right, yeah, I thought of that," I said, totally embarrassed that I had forgotten my *own* superpower.

Slowly and carefully, I made a sturdy staircase of very stale sandwiches and climbed up, slipping through the open window and collapsing onto the ground outside.

"Where are we?" I asked, looking around.

"Just outside Town Hall," Jimmy replied.

"How in the world did you find me here?" I asked, amazed.

"You're not gonna believe this," Jimmy said, lowering his voice to a hushed whisper. "At first, I watched you follow Robot Sophia inside—" He paused, eyeing me carefully. "You *did* realize she was being controlled, right?"

I grunted and told Jimmy to hurry up the story.

"Okay, well, a few minutes later Dr. Vile came out the door. He was seriously coughing, and he went straight over to his machine and was searching desperately for something. Then he pulled out a blue vial, drank it, and fell asleep."

So that's where Dr. Vile was the whole time, I thought to myself.

Jimmy continued. "I decided you were in danger and left the fort. As I was walking around Town Hall, I heard someone talking to a—a—*chicken*. I know it sounds crazy. But I just didn't want that chicken to suffer. So I ran toward the voice, and that's when I found you!"

"And did you find the—uh—chicken whisperer?" I said nervously, sweat building on my cheeks.

"Hmmm, no," Jimmy said in a low voice, his eyes darting around for the mysterious meat-eater.

Whew, that was close, I thought.

CHAPTER 7

A BAD REACTION

Moments later we were running on the freshly cut grass around Town Hall. Unfortunately, the automatic sprinklers were on, and Jimmy and I started slipping and sliding in pools of water.

"How—long—has—this—water—been—on—for?" Jimmy asked, plunging headfirst into a mini ocean and belly flopping so bad that a five-foot wave knocked me over.

"I don't know, but my mom's gonna kill me for getting these shoes wet," I shouted back.

I helped Jimmy up, and we both turned to run.

Suddenly there was a green flash, and Jimmy screamed, "*Green goo!* Run for it!"

But this time, I was ready. Something about the crazy sprinklers had alerted me to danger. I mean, only Dr. Vile would waste water like that.

I ducked, and the goo flew over my head and slammed into a wall behind me. Then there was another green explosion, and a crazy laugh, and that's when I saw Dr. Vile. He was standing on the front steps of Town Hall, mashing his zapper. Still dodging green goo, I rolled behind a bush and waited for my chance.

After yet another wave of goo, I sprang out, firing PB&J sandwiches as hard as I could at the evil scientist.

Honestly, I kinda surprised myself. I saw myself in slow motion, and it was awesome: sandwiches were flying out my hands way faster than I expected, and they were much bigger than anything I had made before.

With a smash, the PB&Js hit their target—Dr. Vile's scrawny little face—and exploded into a mess worse than a kindergarten snack time. As Jimmy fell into another puddle behind me, I watched and waited.

Dr. Vile was coughing hard. In a panic, he peeled the sandwiches off his face and turned to leave. As Jimmy and

I huddled together like soaked ducks, I could still hear the scientist coughing and wheezing in the distance.

"Let's get back to the fort and make a plan. Oh, and by the way, here's your cat back," I said as I handed Jimmy the picture of Lucky George. "Not so lucky after all, huh?"

Jimmy didn't say anything. He just kissed the photo and carefully put it back in his pocket.

CHAPTER 8

THE TRAP

By the time we made it back to our fort in the woods, the sun was high above our heads and shining strong. It was going to be another hot afternoon in Goodsprings.

Jimmy, still trying to get the water out of his ears, was busy solving the mystery about Dr. Vile. "I mean, just *think* about it, PB&J! He sneezes and coughs anytime he's around you—anytime he even talks about you, actually. And when you hit him in the face with that sandwich—"

I finished his thought for him. "He could barely breathe."

Jimmy stopped dead in his tracks. "Wait—do you think that he's allergic to *peanut butter*?"

Suddenly, everything made so much sense. "I think so! Like when Sophia and Dr. Vile caught me in Town Hall, I shot a bunch of PB&Js right into the ceiling—and the scientist wheezed like crazy!"

Jimmy finished my thought. "The blue vial he drank was probably medication to neutralize his allergic reaction!"

I nodded, though I wasn't sure I had understood Jimmy the Walking Dictionary. "English for small children, please."

Jimmy laughed. "That means," he said very slowly, as if talking to a toddler, "he has to take special medicine just to get anywhere near you."

"So, if he's allergic to me," I said carefully, piecing it all together, "then while Dr. Vile is trying to control everyone with food, I can control *him* with *my* superpower?"

Jimmy grinned. "Your superpower isn't so lame anymore, is it?"

I looked down at my hands, truly proud of my sandwich powers for the first time ever.

As we came into the clearing near our fort, Jimmy suddenly put up his hand in alarm and hunched down. "What's the matter?" I asked, on guard. I expected to see Dr. Vile on one of his tanks crashing through the woods at us.

"It's your mom and dad," Jimmy said. "They're standing over there by the fort."

"Oh, great! " I replied, honestly relieved to see my parents. "We can tell them what we know about Dr. Vile.

Maybe they can help us out!" I rolled my eyes and added, "Just watch out for the *death hug.*"

Jimmy didn't seem as excited as me, but I ignored him and ran up to my parents.

"Oh, Christolpherson!" my mother sighed with relief. "You're safe!"

"Son, wanna come inside the fort? We've got some cookies and milk to celebrate. Then you can tell us how you escaped from Dr. Vile!" said Dad.

"Cookies and milk? Awesome!" I replied, running in and reaching greedily for the plate of still-warm cookies and ice-cold milk.

"PB&J . . ." Jimmy started to say, but my mom interrupted him.

"Jimmy, come on now, honey! We have your favorite too. Root-beer floats and potato chips on the side!" My mother's voice was high and excited, almost like it was Christmas morning and she was Santa Claus, handing out presents to all the good girls and boys.

"PB&J, just stop for a second—" Jimmy said again. I ignored him and reached for a cookie.

"Jimmy, look! We're safe now. I mean, we're with my mom and dad." I held the cookie in my hands. It was so warm and soft and smelled delicious. "All that superhero work has to pay off sometime," I added.

"PB&J! Drop that cookie!" Jimmy shouted, and I was so surprised that it fell straight into the milk, splashing over my face and up my nose. Snorting, I heard him whisper in my ear (which was also now covered in milk), "How did your parents know that we escaped from Dr. Vile?"

Suddenly, I knew he was right. *It was a trap!* I looked at my mom and dad. Come to think of it, their smiles were *too* fake. I knew now that they were also being controlled by Dr. Vile, and he was using them to trap us. One bite, and I would have been under his spell forever!

"Jimmy—*RUN!*" I shouted at the top of my lungs, and I pushed the table over, spilling the milk and cookies everywhere.

SUPERHERO TIP #9: SOMETIMES THE ONLY WAY TO ESCAPE A STICKY SITUATION IS TO KNOCK OVER THE STICKY SITUATION.

My parents' smiles suddenly evaporated, and they ran to block the exit. Jimmy got there first, but just as he was running out the door, Robot Dad grabbed me by the shirt. I yelped for help, milk still snorting from my nose. "Jimmyyy!"

Jimmy hesitated at the door, then dove at my father, latching onto his leg and biting him in the thigh. Robot Dad shrieked and let go of me.

"Sorry, Mr. Rederson!" Jimmy said, as Robot Mom ran to help defend her robot husband. Jimmy shouted to me, "Run for it! Leave me here! Use your superpower to defeat Dr. Vile!"

I turned to run, but hesitated. I couldn't do this on my own. I didn't believe in my superpower—I mean, could making sandwiches really save the world? "Jimmy, I can't do this! I'm not ready!"

Jimmy, who was now being tickled by Robot Mom to stop biting Robot Dad, had time for one last word of advice in between mouthfuls: "Go start a food fight!"

The last thing I saw was Robot Mom trying to force a cookie into Jimmy's mouth.

I was officially on my own. It was only me and Dr. Vile. And Jimmy was right. If Dr. Vile wanted to control the world through food, then my PB&Js might just be the answer.

CHAPTER 9

STALE BREAD

After leaving the fort, I headed straight for the middle of town. There, I recorded a fifteen-second video on my phone and pretended to surrender to Dr. Vile.

"Citizens of Goodsprings," I said. I had just plastered peanut butter and jelly on my face (an easy thing to do when you have an infinite supply). I looked like someone had dragged me through the mud and then let a class of toddlers marker all over my face. "I, Christolpherson Rederson, boy superhero, hereby surrender to Dr. Vile. He will find me downtown at noon. Thank you to all my fans (if they exist). Goodbye."

I watched the clip several times and decided a few tears at the end might make it more interesting. I recorded myself sobbing and, once everything was edited together, added a bonus scene of me falling onto my knees in despair. Then I uploaded the clip and waited.

It was noon. The center of town was strangely quiet yet again, as if even the birds knew that the evil scientist was lurking nearby.

And then, I heard it. As I watched, his machine rolled down Main Street and came to a sudden stop right in town square. I held my breath.

Over the loudest microphone I had ever heard came the voice of Dr. Vile.

"PB&Spray, put down your weapons, aka your *hands*, and come out where I can see you."

In response, I slowly walked out, hands up in surrender. Dr. Vile screamed, "I SAID, *HANDS DOWN!*"

I smiled. I liked making him feel nervous, even if I was just a boy superhero with the weirdest superpower ever.

From where I was standing now, I could see the evil scientist's head just above the goo-blasting nozzle of his machine. Slowly lowering my hands, I shouted out, "Oh, afraid of these?" Quick as a flash, my hands were out in front of me, and—I even surprised myself—I fired off the biggest PB&J sandwich the world has ever seen. It was the size of a small car, and it was flying right at Dr. Vile's face.

The scientist screamed and ducked as the sandwich narrowly missed him and slammed into the post office, making a sandwich-shaped hole in the brick. Jelly was dripping everywhere. Still stunned at my own strength, I didn't see Dr. Vile disappear into the machine and lower the nozzle.

Suddenly, a flash of green light hit the telephone pole beside me, which immediately turned it into a pile of steaming roast beef. *Delicious*, I thought, before realizing that *I* could have been that beef. Dr. Vile wasn't trying to *feed* me—he was trying to *cook* me!

SUPERHERO TIP #10: TRY HARD NOT TO GET TURNED INTO BEEF.

Well, I wasn't going to become his dinner. I sprang to life, firing off a quick round of ten sandwiches that dented the side of his machine. Dr. Vile was coming closer now and moving faster and faster until he was definitely breaking the 15-miles-an-hour speed limit. But it was all part of my plan.

Just when the machine was close enough that I could read the sticker "Made in China," I let loose a stale mega sandwich that landed right underneath the machine's wheels.

I had always enjoyed making stale PB&Js as a joke on Jimmy when he was hungry, just to watch his teeth clang down on rock-hard toast. But I never imagined that crusty bread could be so powerful.

Moving fast, Dr. Vile never had a chance to get out of the way—the machine nailed the sandwich and flew up over my head, crashing with a lovely thud right into the side of the bank. Stuck halfway up the three-story building, suddenly it caught on fire and blew Dr. Vile right out onto the steps of Town Hall. He groaned and lay back, touching his head and moaning, "Oh, Mommy . . . Mommy . . ."

And that's when I saw it lying on the ground—*the remote!*

CHAPTER 10

FIRE AND SMOKE

The remote was lying a few feet away from Dr. Vile. Without his machine or remote, the scientist was basically a nobody—just a scrawny loser with flabby arms. If I could just get to it first!

Dr. Vile, still dizzy from the shock, somehow also noticed that his zapper was gone, and sprang to his feet, looking desperately in every direction. I raised my hands and nailed him with a PB&J right in the tummy, but it wasn't enough. He reached the remote—and yes, I hate to say it, but the crazy laughter started again.

"You thought you could defeat me, boy?" Dr. Vile screamed in a squeaky voice.

I didn't have time to talk. I dropped to a knee and blasted an assortment of PB&Js at him, but this time it didn't work. He ducked down, using the remote to fire green goo into the sandwiches. They immediately turned to pudding and fell helplessly to the steps below. I sent another round of sandwiches, but it was just no use.

Think, think, think! I said to myself as I ducked from a blast of green goo. *What would Jimmy do right now?*

At first all I could think of was Jimmy's bad haircut, but then an idea hit me like a snowball on Christmas Day.

SUPERHERO TIP #11: IF POSSIBLE, ALWAYS BEAT THE BAD GUY BEFORE CHRISTMAS BREAK. THAT WAY YOU CAN ENJOY YOUR VACATION IN PEACE.

I turned and ran away from Dr. Vile. He laughed, shouting, "Run, boy! Run for your life! I am lord of Goodsprings, and soon I will become lord of the universe! Ahahaha!"

But I was ignoring him now. I reached the bank. High above me was Dr. Vile's ruined machine, still stuck halfway up and engulfed in flames. I raised my hands and did my

magic—sending   tens—no,   *hundreds*—of   PB&J
sandwiches up at the fire as fast as I could launch them.

Dr. Vile was still laughing as he crossed the street.
"*Hmmm*, afraid of a little fire, PB&Spray? Or scared of what
Mayor Lumford will say when he finds out you burnt his
town's bank to the ground?!"

Knowing I had only seconds for my plan to work, I sent
even more sandwiches into the flames above my head. The
smoke, which was blowing straight over Main Street, was
everywhere now and so thick I could hardly see the
buildings across the street. I ducked down to avoid the
black fumes and kept doing my work.

"It's time for you to take your medicine, boy," said the
ugly scientist in a sickly-sweet voice. "What would you like
for dinner?" With that, he fired a shot of green goo into the
car parked beside me, which immediately evaporated into
a bowl of chicken-noodle soup.

Trying desperately to keep calm, I decided to play
along.

"*Ugh*, no! Not soup! That's so yucky," I answered back, trying to imitate Sophia Little's sassiest voice.

"Well, WHAT THEN?!" screamed Dr. Vile. Suddenly everywhere around me were flashes of green light and plates of food. "You see, boy, I don't want to turn you into dessert. I want to control you. I need you so that I can control the universe." He paused from firing the goo and looked up into the sky as he daydreamed about ruling the galaxy. "I need . . . a superhero . . . under my control . . ."

Just at that moment, I knew my plan had worked. Dr. Vile, now almost completely lost in the smoke, started coughing and couldn't stop.

"What . . . have . . . you . . . done?" Dr. Vile screamed in choking fits.

"You're allergic to peanut butter, dear old doctor! Well, burnt sandwiches are better than no sandwiches at all. This smoke is filled with millions and millions of peanut molecules!" I shouted.

"NOOOO!" he screamed. Dr. Vile reached for his microphone and in the loudest voice he could, shrieked, "Help, *Sophia*! Save me!"

In spooky-fast time—I mean, less than two seconds— Robot Sophia appeared on the steps, running to save the scientist from his allergic reaction. She was holding a special tube filled with blue liquid, and I looked on, helpless, as he took it and drank it all.

Dr. Vile let the tube fall to the ground, then stood up. The blue liquid had worked. The peanut allergy wouldn't bother him anymore today.

CHAPTER 11

LEMON-CREAM PIE

There they were—Dr. Vile and Robot Sophia, his evil sidekick. In a strange way, I actually felt bad for Sophia, knowing that she was being controlled by such an evil scientist with strange green goo. But then I remembered her sassy attitude, and I didn't feel so bad anymore.

"Now it's time for your destiny," said Dr. Vile.

"Fat chance," I said. "You'll have to turn me into a lemon-cream pie if you want to take over the galaxy!" I love lemon-cream pie and was hoping he would miss me and make a big one for later.

SUPERHERO TIP #12: ALWAYS USE THE BAD GUY'S POWER TO YOUR ADVANTAGE. IF YOU'RE NOT SURE HOW TO DO THAT, JUST ASK HIM FOR LEMON-CREAM PIE.

"So be it, pie boy," he said, pressing the button.

I covered my face and waited for the goo to hit me. I wasn't sure what being turned into pie felt like, but I hoped that it would be tasty.

After a second or two, I looked up, wondering if pies could think thoughts, when I realized nothing had happened. There, standing in front of me holding a big piece of cardboard and wearing a bicycle helmet with two antennas on top, was Jimmy!

"Jimmy!" I shouted, hugging my friend. "How did you get away from the Robot Parents?" Then I screamed. "Wait—are you *Robot* Jimmy now?"

"I just kept biting Robot Dad's leg," he said. "I hope that's okay."

I wanted to squish him and say, "That's amazing!" but this was no time for celebration.

Dr. Vile angrily raised his zapper to strike again. Now that I had Jimmy back on my side, I knew we couldn't lose.

"Team PB&J forever!" I shouted. I raised my hands, and hundreds of mini sandwiches flew out from my palms. And when I say mini, I mean it—some were the size of flies and zipped right up Dr. Vile's nostrils. His really gross nostrils, I might add.

The scientist had met his match. The green goo couldn't zap all of the super tiny sandwiches.

Angrily, he turned and ran toward Town Hall, dragging Sophia behind him and using her to block the flying bread. I saw PB&Js knocking into her noggin, and I actually laughed out loud.

"Knock the remote from his hands, PB&J!" shouted Jimmy.

In one last surge of power, hundreds of sandwiches poured out of my hands. They all flew right at the remote, and finally it happened. A mega PB&J smashed into Dr. Vile's left hand, and it tumbled down the steps toward us.

"Jimmy, grab the zapper thingy!" I screamed. Jimmy tried to reach it, but he tripped on the first step and fell, banging up his shin and crying out the strangest "Oogghoogh" I had ever heard. He really did sound like a sick hippo.

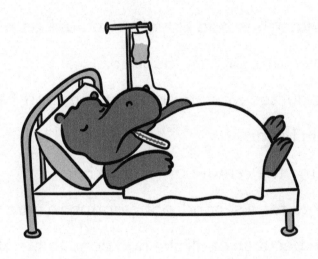

SUPERHERO TIP #13: PRACTICE MAKING MANLY GRUNTS WHEN YOU GET HURT. THAT WAY THE BAD GUY DOESN'T LAUGH AT YOU TOO MUCH WHEN YOU FALL DOWN.

Jimmy's fall was a real mess, and to make matters worse, random widgets and gadgets from his pockets spilled all over the ground and went flying in every direction.

Knowing I had to focus and get the zapper, I stopped firing my sandwiches and dove for it. Just as my fingers touched the remote, Dr. Vile laughed.

The evil doctor was standing at the top of the stairs with Sophia in his arms.

"Throw me the remote or I'll drop her!"

I hesitated for a second, not wanting to care too much about Sophia because of all she had done to me. But I knew that the fall would be a big ouchy for her, and I couldn't just let her tumble like that.

Just then, the wind whipped up Jimmy's picture of his lucky cat, George, launching it up the steps and right smack dab into Dr. Vile's face. For a second there was silence, but then all I could hear was him screaming. In the weirdest cute-kitty panic ever, he let go of Sophia and scratched at his face, trying to destroy the photo as fast as he could.

With lightning speed, I shot out a mattress-sized PB&J on the softest white bread I could imagine, and Sophia fell with a thud right into it and disappeared deep in the jelly. I breathed a sigh of relief and turned toward Dr. Vile. Jimmy was thankfully done with his hippo noises and standing at my side again.

"As for you, Lord Vile," I said triumphantly, "wanna sandwich?"

Dr. Vile had just removed the kitty photo and was staring down at us blankly.

Then, just like that, a massive pile of hundreds of sandwiches fell from the sky and trapped him in a cage of crusty old bread, with peanut butter for cement. Jimmy and I together smashed the remote, fell down in exhaustion, and waited for the rest of the town to show up.

Jimmy looked over at me. "You DID it, PB&J!"

"No," I said. "*Team PB&J* did it."

CHAPTER 12

TEAM PB&J

As you can imagine, life changed a lot after Jimmy and I defeated ol' Dr. Vile. For one thing, everyone around town started calling me PB&J instead of that *other* name (I don't want to say it again, but you know which one I'm talking about).

Amazingly, Jimmy got his cat photo back, and it wasn't damaged at all.

I guess George really *is* one lucky kitty.

SUPERHERO TIP #14: TRY YOUR BEST TO HAVE A LUCKY CAT. A LUCKY GOLDFISH COULD ALSO WORK, BUT SOMEBODY'S LUCKY CAT WILL PROBABLY EAT IT.

Sophia Little and I became good friends, and not only because I saved her from the stairs of death. As it turns out, she just doesn't like jelly that much (weird, I know, but whatever). So now I know to make her only dry peanut-butter sandwiches, which is kinda weird if you ask me, and definitely not something to be *sassy* about, but still, it's good to be friends.

Jimmy and I are really famous around Goodsprings now. In our victory parade, Mr. Malinski—father of Blaze Malinski, the seed spitter—drove us around in his pick-up truck all decorated with glitter and pink, girly letters that his daughter Angela had written in chalk. It looked weird, but hey, I'm not complaining.

That was an interesting parade. Everywhere we went, people were screaming and asking me to hit them with PB&J sandwiches. It all started with one guy who ran out into the road in front of the pick-up truck.

"Yo, PB-man, bury me in jelly, dude!"

"Okay . . ." I responded, not sure what was happening, but happy that someone appreciated my powers. And boy, did I cover him good. That guy was in jelly heaven for weeks.

Oh, and yeah, my parents are back to normal now, which is good, since having robotic parents controlled by an evil lord is never good. Jimmy apologized for biting my dad's leg, too. Normally I would say Jimmy didn't have to, but after I saw the mark he left, I think it was the only decent thing to do.

Dr. Vile was taken away to a state prison by our dear old security guards, Ron and Phil, who were promised Free-Donut Fridays again as soon as the town was cleaned up. As for the evil scientist himself, after we figured out he was afraid of kittens, the only answer was to make him work at the state animal shelter, where all day long he donates his time to caring for cute, cuddly felines.

In my spare time as a kid superhero, I now practice my powers at the new facility that Mayor Lumford built for Jimmy, Sophia, and me. It's pretty sweet. Jimmy developed some new virtual villains for me to defeat, one of which is a hungry hippo (I just feed him . . . it's easy). Jimmy also tracks my progress using his sick computer software. Next time a bad guy invades Goodsprings, we'll be ready.

Today at practice, Sophia dropped by to watch us practice. Jimmy got nervous, tripped over a pile of computer parts, and fell into a barrel of spare jelly. We all laughed, and after he licked himself off, we sat outside on the front steps and ate fresh PB&J sandwiches with plum jelly, a new recipe I was experimenting with.

"You know," said Sophia, "I underestimated your superpower, PB&J. I have to admit—you kinda impressed me when you defeated Dr. Vile." But then, a little embarrassed, she quickly added, "But this plum stuff is gross." Still as sassy as ever. "Just stick to the strawberry kind, okay?"

I nodded, agreeing with her. Then I asked them, "Guys, do you think we should try a green-goo flavor sometime?"

"Noooooo!" they both replied.

THANKS FOR SAVING THE DAY WITH YOUR REVIEWS!

Congratulations! You read this book all the way through. I really hope it was exciting and made you **laugh**. Wasn't it amazing when PB&J and Jimmy teamed up to defeat Dr. Vile and rid the world of green goo? And how they made a new friend along the way?

Anyway, there are lots of books out there, and sometimes it's hard to find one you enjoy. Hopefully my book really made your day (and made you *hungry* too! Snack time, anyone?).

I wanted to ask for your **superhero help** by leaving a review. It should only take five minutes, and it doesn't have to be written like Jimmy the Dictionary either!

Thanks for your help. I'll do my best to keep making these books funny, exciting, and—you guessed it—snackish for you all!

Until next time!

Your PB&J Author,

Jon Haney

Printed in Great Britain
by Amazon